KATE'S GIANTS

For Holly ~ *V. G.*

The best in this kind are but shadows,
and the worst are no worse,
if imagination amend them.
—William Shakespeare, *A Midsummer Night's Dream*

For C. M. ~ *V. A.*

Text copyright © 1995 by Valiska Gregory
Illustrations copyright © 1995 by Virginia Austin

First U.S. paperback edition 1997

The Library of Congress has cataloged the hardcover edition as follows:

Gregory, Valiska.
Kate's giants / Valiska Gregory ; illustrated by Virginia Austin.—1st U.S. ed.
Summary: Kate is frightened that things like giants might sneak through
the attic door into her new room, until she learns that what she can think
up she can think out too.
ISBN 1-56402-299-4 (hardcover)
[1. Giants—Fiction. 2. Fear of the dark—Fiction.]
I. Austin, Virginia, date, ill. II. Title
PZ7.G8624Kat   1995
[E]—dc20   95-6303

ISBN 0-7636-0151-9 (paperback)

10 9 8 7 6 5 4 3 2 1

Printed in Hong Kong

This book was typeset in Garamond Condensed.
The pictures were done in pencil and watercolor.

Candlewick Press
2067 Massachusetts Avenue
Cambridge, Massachusetts 02140

KATE'S GIANTS

Valiska Gregory

illustrated by **Virginia Austin**

CANDLEWICK PRESS
CAMBRIDGE, MASSACHUSETTS

In Kate's new room there was a door,
small and curious as Kate herself.
"It's the door to the attic," said her parents.

But Kate didn't like it.
"What if scary things come through
that door?" she said.

**And sure enough,
when Kate was tucked in tight,**

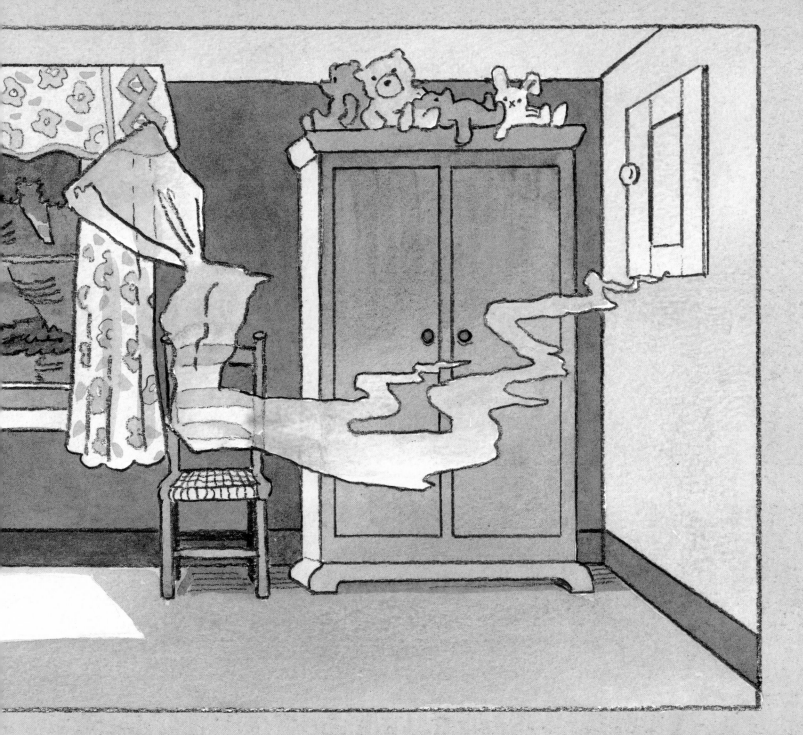

**and shadows moved like fingers on the wall,
she thought they did.**

Shifting shapes in the dark, they waited and watched, and just as they slithered around her bed, Kate covered her eyes and yelled,

"HELP!"

Her father said, "If you can think them up,
then you can think them out."
"It won't be easy," said Kate.

She saw a tree move its witchy hand.
"What if animals come through
that door?" she said.

And sure enough, when Kate was all alone,

she thought she heard a scritching sound—

a lion with teeth as sharp
as claws, two hungry bears
with lumbering paws.
They growled and they
roared so loud, that she
could barely call out,

" H E L P ! "

Her mother said, "If you can think them up,
then you can think them out.
Just take a deep breath before you think."

Kate heard thunder rumbling the panes.
"But what if giants come through
that door?" she said.

And sure enough, as Kate sat in the dark,

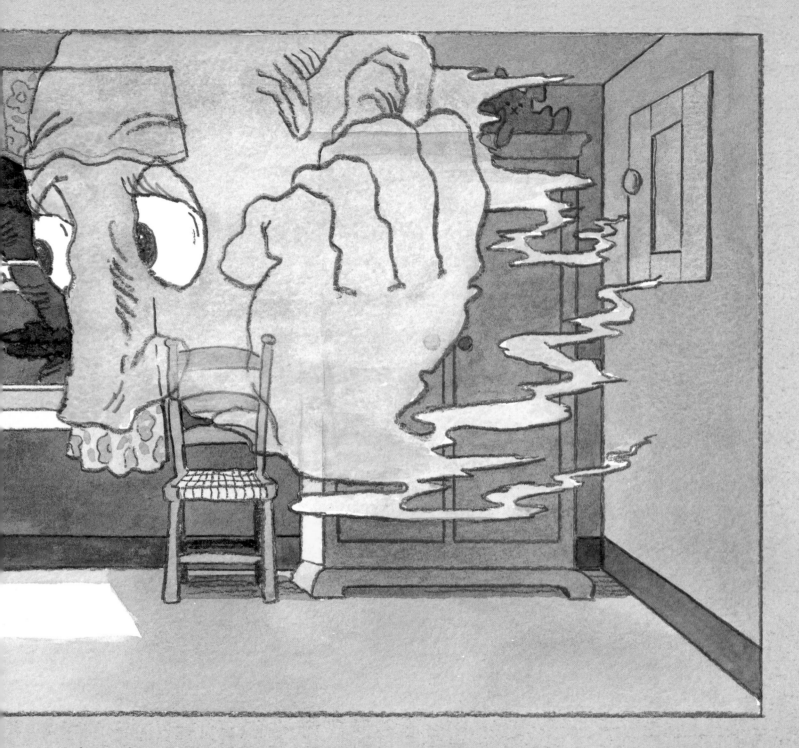

she thought she saw them come.

Two giants squeezed in so tall
and so fat there was barely
room for their marmalade cat.
But this time Kate knew
just what to do—she took
a deep breath and said,

"STOP! If I can think you up,

then I can think you out."

And sure enough, she did.

Outside the window,
the moon was round
as an owl's eye.

Kate thought about the attic door.
"I wonder if friendly things could come through
that door," she said.

And sure enough, she thought they did.

Kate smiled a friendly giant smile.
"This is the best part," she said.

"If I can think them out,
then sometimes, I can think them in!"